For Maddie, Piper and Riley - K.C.

For the wonderful Steyning Bookshop - N.S.

BLOOMSBURY CHILDREN'S BOOKS
Bloomsbury Publishing Plc
50 Bedford Square, London, WC1B 3DP, UK

BLOOMSBURY, BLOOMSBURY CHILDREN'S BOOKS and the Diana logo are
trademarks of Bloomsbury Publishing Plc

First published in Great Britain 2020 by Bloomsbury Publishing Plc

Text copyright © Katrina Charman 2020
Illustrations copyright © Nick Sharratt 2020

Katrina Charman and Nick Sharratt have asserted their rights under the Copyright,
Designs and Patents Act, 1988, to be identified as the Author and Illustrator of this work

A catalogue record for this book is available from the British Library

ISBN: HB: 978 1 5266 0344 9 • PB: 978 1 5266 0343 2 • eBook: 978 1 5266 0342 5

2 4 6 8 10 9 7 5 3 1
Printed and bound in China by Leo Paper Products, Heshan, Guangdong

All papers used by Bloomsbury Publishing Plc are natural, recyclable products
from wood grown in well managed forests. The manufacturing
processes conform to the environmental regulations of the country of origin

To find out more about our authors and books visit
www.bloomsbury.com and sign up for our newsletters

Search, renew or reserve
www.buckinghamshire.gov.uk/libraries

24 hour renewal line
0303 123 0035

Library enquiries
01296 382415

Buckinghamshire Libraries and Culture

#loveyourlibrary

@BucksLibraries

The Whales
on the
Bus

Katrina Charman   Nick Sharratt

BLOOMSBURY
CHILDREN'S BOOKS
LONDON OXFORD NEW YORK NEW DELHI SYDNEY

The whales on the bus
ride round the town,

round the town,

round the town.

The cranes on the train
cry choo, choo, choo!

Choo, choo, choo!

Choo, choo, choo!

The bees on their skis go

zoom, zoom, zoom!

Zoom, zoom, zoom!

Zoom, zoom, zoom!

The bees
on their skis go
zoom, zoom, zoom!
all day long.

The sheep in the jeep
race through the mud,

all day long.

The seals on the sub
dive up and down,

up and down,

up and down.

The seals
on the sub
dive up
and down,

all day long.

The tiger in the glider
does loop-the-loops,

loop-the-loops,

loop-the-loops.

The tiger in the glider
does
loop-the-loops,

all day long.

The ducks on the truck go

quack,
  quack,
    beep!

quack,
  quack,
    beep!

quack,
  quack,
    beep!

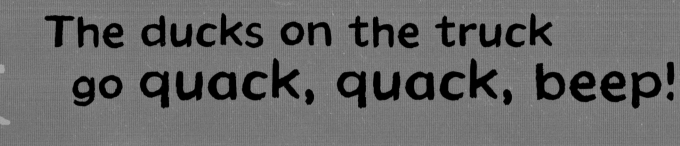

The ducks on the truck
go quack, quack, beep!

all day long.

The goat on the boat
sings Yo ho ho!

Yo ho ho!

Yo ho ho!

The goat
on the boat
sings **yo ho ho!**
all day long.

The snakes on skates
go slip and slide,

slip and slide,

slip and slide.

The baboons in balloons
float home for tea,

home for tea,
home for tea.